Horror S
To Tell In The Dark

BOOK 3

SHORT SCARY ANTHOLOGY FOR TEENAGERS AND YOUNG ADULTS

BRYCE NEALHAM

HORROR STORIES TO TELL IN THE DARK: BOOK 3

Copyright © by Bryce Nealham.

All rights reserved. No part of this publication may be reproduced, distributed, or transmitted in any form or by any means, including photocopying, recording, or other electronic or mechanical methods, or by any information storage and retrieval system without the prior written permission of the publisher, except in the case of very brief quotations embodied in critical reviews and certain other noncommercial uses permitted by copyright law.

This is a work of fiction. Names, characters, business, events and incidents are the products of the author's imagination. Any resemblance to actual persons, living or dead, or actual events is purely coincidental.

HORROR STORIES TO TELL IN THE DARK: BOOK 3

CONTENTS

SUSTENANCE 1
    Frederick Trinidad 11
THE DEMON OF PENITENT HIGH 1
    J. R. Gawne 9
WHERE THE DEAD LIE 11
    Maya Scianna 20
ELSEWHERE 21
    Daniel Okotete 33
DRINKS PROVIDED 35
    Coward Huntington 45
THE BESTSELLER 47
    David Phiri 55

HORROR STORIES TO TELL IN THE DARK: BOOK 3

Find Out About Our Latest Horror Book Releases...

Simply go to the URL below and you will be notified as soon as a new book has been launched.

bit.ly/3q34yte

> "O little one,
>
> My little one,
>
> Come with me,
>
> Your life is done.
>
> Forget the future,
>
> Forget the past.
>
> Life is over:
>
> Breathe your last."
>
> — Clive Barker

SUSTENANCE

By Frederick Trinidad

That night was humid and the air offered no breeze. Yet, cold sweat dripped from my head and run through my spine.

I stood at a corner, anxiously waiting for someone so I could go home and get it over with.

A man approached me and our hands exchanged money. It was my wages for the night's work.

The amount I received for a single night's work amounted to much more than a month's worth of salary from my previous jobs. That was the first of a series of jobs I did for the company.

What was the job?

It was a simple clean-up job.

But, I shouldn't have taken it because I couldn't stomach the sight of severed limbs.

In the previous months prior to working there, I used to work as a janitor at a prestigious hotel. I've been working there for many years then but they had to lay people off due to loss of business as a result of the Covid-19 pandemic.

Yes, I'm one of those who lost their jobs due to the damn virus.

From then on, I worked odd jobs here and there, just basically trying to survive.

But as of late, jobs were far in between and when I do find one, the pay was always next to nothing. The bills were piling up, the fridge was empty save for a half jar of mustard, and my eviction notice was past due.

I was desperate, to say the least.

One day, I bumped into Billy. He was having lunch on the patio of a mid-class restaurant. The guy was just as impoverished as me but there he was; finely clothed and was eating a decent sandwich.

He saw me walking by the street and gestured for me to approach him. I must've looked like a homeless wanderer who approached him hoping for alms.

He asked me to join him at his table then ordered me a sandwich. We get to talking and later went down to business.

He's been working as a clean-up crew and the company pays very well. The work happens only once a week so he gets to spend a lot of time and money on his personal endeavors.

He then plainly revealed that the work is cleaning up the remains of dead people. There will be a primary crew whose job is to remove the remains of the dead and our task is to clean up after them.

He told me they were currently shorthanded and in fact, he'll receive a handsome incentive by referring others. I deduced right away that our job was to clean up after the dirty work of the mafia.

At first, I was reluctant about working the shady job but I ultimately agreed due to obvious financial reasons.

The first job happened in an abandoned warehouse. We were

allowed entry long after the first crew removed the bodies.

Then, I was given the first taste of the gruesome scene.

The floor was covered in blood and there were splashes of blood upon the wall. I never thought of myself as squeamish but the sheer amount of blood and the way they're splattered in utter disarray was enough to give me nightmares.

The heavy metallic smell of blood persistently clogged my nose. On one of the first strokes I did with the cleaning brush, the bristles caught what looked like a fresh clump of hair connected to an inch of skin. I almost puked at the sight.

Worst still, not far from the clump of hair, was a severed finger with the bone protruding from its lopped opening. I gasped at the horrible sight and stepped aside for a moment in order to collect myself.

"Hey Billy, this idiot knows what the job is right?" One of the armed minders who were wearing a gas mask questioned Billy as he was visibly annoyed with my constant retching.

Billy let go of his mop, walked over to me then handed me a chewing mint gum.

"Just make it through the first few jobs and you'll get used to it." Billy assured me.

Sure enough, the more I did it, the more it became just another job.

I've soon gotten used to all manner of blood activity and all sorts of severed body parts. The cleanup always occurs within abandoned warehouses and we were made to be there about a quarter of an hour after the bodies were taken out.

We were never allowed to even see the bodies.

We were never even told who we were working for.

Although one time, I saw a faded but discernible logo on one of their vehicles. It was the Birschmark corporate logo.

A group of huge Russian conglomerates who builds monumental malls, airports, and hotels throughout the world. It never really mattered to us anyway, as long as they keep paying us well.

We were called and let in at precisely the right moment, all the time. Billy and the other cleanup guys never cared to know more than what they're allowed. They were just happy enough to do the cleanup and bring home a healthy wad of cash.

But my curiosity got the better of me and I started asking questions. One of the peculiarities I noticed was the lack of bullet casings at every scene.

If these were mob hits, you'd expect some shells here and there but there was none.

Sure, they could've used knives or other melee weapons for the hits but still, the complete lack of arsenal evidence bothered me.

As you'd expect, I first asked Billy about it but he didn't give me anything. Instead, he warned me that grave consequences await those who go beyond minding their own fucking business. But a part of me just couldn't brush it off; I had to know more.

We were always called in for the job every Wednesday evening, it never failed. The abandoned warehouses were not very far from each other.

Having nothing better to do, every Wednesday night, I scouted the warehouses not far from the previous locations and would hang around there and wait to be called in for the job.

Nothing came off of my first 2 scouting expeditions. However, I finally achieved my goal on the 3rd. I was loitering outside a warehouse when 3 vehicles drove into the property.

I ran and hid behind some thick bush, careful not to be spotted by any of those vehicles.

There were 2 SUVs and a huge container truck. Armed men wearing gas masks alighted the SUVs along with a group of bound men and women.

Along with a few lighting equipment, the armed men led the captives into the warehouse. The container truck made a loud banging noise from the inside.

Then the truck started positioning its rear end towards the opening of the warehouse, as the armed men exited the building.

I moved from the bush to look into one of the warehouse's rear windows. I didn't know yet but I was about to witness the most horrific scene I have ever encountered.

What I thought was a simple cleanup after a mob hit turned out to be something a lot more sinister.

There was never an initial cleanup crew that removed the bodies. In fact, there were no bodies left to begin with.

The captives consisting of 2 men and women were bound and left seating on the floor. They were sobbing but paused to hold their breaths as the container began to open its door, unraveling the monstrosity that lied within.

A humanoid beast presented itself.

The creature was about 15 feet tall and its muscular body was covered in fizzy, knotted gray hair.

It carries the face of an ape, with rows of long jagged teeth in its mouth like those of a great white shark. Visibly famished, the beast dashed towards the helpless victims.

All of them were too shocked and panic-stricken to move from the spot, making it easy for the beast to bury its fangs upon one of the men's heads.

In just one swift move of its body, the beast nastily decapitated the man and proceeded to eat his head, and quickly moved to consume the rest of his body.

All this was happening in plain view of the others, knowing full well that they're going to be next.

The beast was still masticating the first victim in its mouth when it dashed for its next meal. This time burying its long sharp claws into one of the women's chests, killing her instantly.

The others watched in horror as they could barely move, frozen down by fear and shock at the fates of those who were killed before them.

All they were able to muster were panicked screams as the monster went through them like a hot knife through butter.

I couldn't watch any more.

My knees weakened and I fell on my ass, still staring up the window.

I no longer have a view of the horrible scene but the horrid screams of the victims coupled with the shadows reflecting from the ceiling continued to show me the movements of the macabre affair that was going on.

A moment passed by and everything was quiet. The beast seemingly devoured all 4 victims in less than 15 minutes. I remained nailed to my hidden spot, still in awe and utter disbelief at what I just witnessed.

I mustered all my strength to stand up once again in order to look through the same window. None of the victims were there, the beast apparently consumed them clean; clothes, bones, and all.

Then all the lights went out.

Red light from what I deduced to be within the container truck started flashing. I then heard a sickening growl from the beast who seemed to have dashed towards the flashing light.

I heard the door of the container slam shut then all the lighting equipment was turned on again. Some of the armed men walked into the building to inspect the bloody scene.

The others rode in one of the SUVs, escorting the container truck as it drove away from the property.

I stepped away from the window and disappeared into the thick bush behind the warehouse.

Try as I might, I could not wrap my head around what just happened. I looked at the naked palm of my hand trying to visualize the blood, flesh, and bones within it.

Unable to avoid imagining that my body could very easily be in place of those devoured victims. Minutes passed by and my phone received the familiar SMS.

It was time for the cleanup crew to arrive and perform their task. What's left of my sanity was trying to convince me not to show up for work that night. To just run away and cut all ties with them.

But, it would raise much suspicion if I didn't show up for work that night. So I decided to try and stay calm and do what was needful.

I remained hidden behind the bush till Billy and the rest of the cleanup crew arrive.

When they arrived, I took a long way around the property so that I would walk in from the road rather than from the rear of the warehouse.

I didn't notice right away but I apparently looked pale and still visibly shaken.

"Sorry, I'm down with the flu today." I reasoned with one of the armed men.

Thereafter, I was sent home without pay but I didn't mind at all. In fact, I was so damn glad to be away from that wretched place.

The following days saw me shutting myself inside my apartment. I rejected all phone calls including the ones from Billy and I avoided getting off the bed altogether.

I grew paranoid at everything, imagining myself being forcibly taken by those armed men to be offered as the beast's next meal.

Each night, I dreamt of the same nightmare. My mind never ceased to picture the likeness of the beast as it devoured those people.

As another Wednesday draws near, I grew ever more weary and comprehensive over the whole situation. I was so distraught and tired of the impending doom that I decided to do something in order to rid myself of the terrible conundrum.

I reported my plight to the police.

The front desk was so confused about the absurdity of my story that I was deemed mentally unstable. But then, I was invited to an interrogation room by one of the detectives.

The room contained a table, several chairs, and a camera connected atop a tripod.

Then we started to talk.

I poured my heart out to him and described the whole thing in every minute detail.

"Wow, that is quite a story." Remarked the bearded police veteran.

I nodded silently, unable to utter words irrelevant to the main narrative. The detective offered me a cup of coffee to which I thoughtlessly accepted.

Then he stepped out of the room and I released a great sigh of relief.

I was in a relatively safe place and for the first time since the horrid experience, I was able to have some feeling of security and comfort.

The detective went back and handed me a warm cup of coffee. My body thankfully sniffed the soothing aroma and the warmth of the drink peacefully embraced my soul.

I was feeling very relaxed at that point.

The detective then moved towards the camera, ejected the memory card, and proceeded to say:

"You really are an idiot. You should've just kept doing your job, kept taking the money, and kept your mouth shut." The detective told me in a very harrowing voice.

I then recalled the previous time someone called me an idiot. It was said by the man wearing a gas mask during my first day of work.

Then I realized that he and the detective shared the same voice. I remember gasping before passing out.

I woke up to the soft humming sound of a modern car engine. Both my hands and feet were bound and I was seated in the backseat of a car.

I still felt woozy but the driver noticed I was already awake.

"Hey just in case you're wondering... we're employed by Birschmark's founder and CEO." the driver told me in a hushed but deliberate tone.

"That thing is rumored to be his son borne from some supernatural bullshit... laughable, ain't it? But who cares? We're not paid to know, we're paid to work and shut up." the driver said as he turned the vehicle into a corner.

Our vehicle then moved to park near a container truck with its rear-end facing the opening of a derelict warehouse. A loud banging sound emanated from within the container.

"Come on, he's hungry." were the very last words ever spoken to me.

ABOUT THE AUTHOR

Frederick Trinidad

Frederick has been in the business of ghostwriting for a couple of years now. He wrote blogs for brands, web articles, social media posts, and scripts for different YouTube channels.

However, writing stories has been his passion since childhood and this anthology is his way of expanding his writing career and reaching a wide range of audiences. He discovered his love for horror storytelling during the peak of the pandemic when the world held its breath amidst a global state of uncertainty.

His innovative style of writing is designed to make readers experience his distinctive brand of horror and mystery for themselves.

Fred wrote a mystery/thriller novel that he works to see published by the first quarter of 2022. The short story contributions that he imparted in this anthology shall give you a peek at the horror that awaits you in that book and his literary works in the future.

To receive updates from his work, you can follow his personal Facebook account at:
https://www.facebook.com/frederick.trinidad.3

You can also reach him via email at: trinidadfred79@gmail.com

THE DEMON OF PENITENT HIGH

By J. R. Gawne

As she walked towards the school in the fading, crimson-and-gold light of dusk, Mia reflected on the events that had brought her here.

"Meet us by the fence out back of the school around five. Be sure to wear something hot." Zoe had told her. *What are her and Ava planning?* Mia wondered nervously.

She thought about how she had seen Ava talking to Mr Kaufman right after class that day and wondered if it had anything to do with what her two friends had planned for tonight.

As she walked, she continued to speculate on the true nature of Ava's relationship to Mr Kaufman. She had seen the two talking a lot the past month or so, and they spoke to each other with a strange familiarity, like they shared some sort of secret.

Mia was startled when she suddenly bumped into someone. She was about to apologize but the words died in her throat when she saw the person she had bumped into was Mr. Kaufman himself, out of his school suit and wearing a more casual dress shirt.

"Ah, Mia, you're in my 6th period history class aren't you?" He said, giving her a slimy smile that sent chills down her spine.

"You'd best be careful young lady, a curvaceous girl like you shouldn't be out after dark without an escort. God forbid something might happen."

His smile while he said that left Mia feeling extremely uncomfortable and she struggled to come up with something to excuse herself.

"Have you finished that analysis on Anne Frank's diary yet?" He asked, almost conversationally. "It's due on Thursday you know."

"Y-yes sir." Mia stammered.

"Good." He said, once more flashing that creepy smile that made Mia's skin crawl. "I look forward to seeing it on my desk."

With that, he moved off away from the school, and Mia was left unnerved by the strange interaction. Nevertheless, she continued towards the school, if only to get as far away from Mr Kaufman as possible.

In the golden brilliance of the setting sun the shadowy, imposing silhouette of the school looked like some kind of ancient stone fortress of oppressive malice as she approached. Not surprising, considering its origin.

Penitent High had started life as an asylum back in the early 1800's, at which point it had been run by the local Catholic church, until a string of gruesome murders within its halls had forced the local government to close it down sometime in the late 1890's.

It had reopened decades later as a prison, but a similar rash of deadly and brutal killings and reoccurring prison riots had left the facility unable to find enough volunteers to keep its guard shifts fully staffed.

Eventually after a guard strike, the prison closed down, and in the early 60's the facility had been converted into a high school serving the town of Greywater and the surrounding area. Since then there had been no incidents of murder or reports of any level of violence beyond the occasional tussle between boys in the schoolyard, although most of the locals stayed away after dark.

The imposing shadow of the massive, blocky building was especially intimidating at night, when its height and bulk were exaggerated by the inky darkness. Mia hoped whatever her friends had planned, it wouldn't take long.

She saw Zoe and Ava standing near the large hole in the fence. As she got closer she saw Ava take something from Zoe and slip it into her purse. It looked like-condoms? *Why would Ava bring condoms to hang out?* She thought to herself. *Is she going to see someone after?*

Mia knew Ava slept around with some of the sports teams and she'd heard rumors that a few of the guys in band class knew what Ava looked like naked. *But why wouldn't she just pick them up after?*

"Mia!" Zoe called out to her, beckoning her over after noticing her approaching from across the street. Mia jogged across the empty road to join the other two girls. She felt a little exposed in her tank top and yoga pants, but it was the only sort of clothing she had that felt "hot." Even if the tank top didn't make her stomach look as flat as she wanted, and the low-cut neck made her feel like her boobs were going to fall out.

She'd thought about buying actual sexy clothes, but she felt that would only encourage Zoe and Ava to keep dragging her out on "excursions" when she'd rather stay at home with a good book.

"Same old same old huh?" Ava teased, poking Mia in the tits.

"Screw you! I'm comfy." Mia replied hiding her irritation behind a facade of friendly banter.

"Its good enough," Zoe said looking her up and down. "the boys are gunna love her."

"Boys?!" Mia's heart jumped. "You didn't tell me we were meeting any boys!" Ava rolled her eyes.

"Oh come on Mia, you gotta live a little!"

"Hey! You three!" The girl's heads turned sharply, and Mia's heart leaped, half in hope, half in fear as she recognized James, the handsome TA from her English class. His long legs ate up the ground as he moved towards them, his arms exposed by the T-shirt he was wearing, revealing the heavily muscled forearms Mia had sometimes dared to imagine wrapped around her on lonely nights.

If he had caught them, maybe this would be it, Zoe and Ava would be forced to give up whatever plans they had for the evening.

"What are you three up to?" James asked Ava, who had already stepped forward as if to make herself the head of the group.

"We're just hanging out." She said with a casual air that Mia knew was a false as her nails and the smile she flashed him. James seemed unaffected by her charms, and pressed the issue.

"Any specific reason why you're hanging out close to that hole in the fence?"

"Just making sure nobody else goes through." Ava replied coolly, with a self-assurance Mia envied. James didn't look like he was buying it, but he didn't have any actual reason, or authority, to make them move.

The sidewalk they were standing on was public, and they weren't technically on school property yet. Mia's heart sank as she realized that Ava and Zoe were about to get away with whatever they had planned for tonight, and were going to drag her along with them.

"Alright." James said, and Mia felt her last hope of escaping this night die at the word. "You girls be careful, the school isn't safe at night." He glanced specifically at Mia as he spoke and their eyes met, she hoped he saw the desperation in hers, and was surprised to see a glimmer of something like real concern in his hazel eyes. The moment passed however, and he walked past them continuing down the street.

Once he turned the corner and was out of sight, Mia turned on Ava. "You didn't say anything about us meeting boys Ava! Is that what the condoms are for?" She was nervous, she was starting to get a good idea of what was going on, and she didn't feel right about it. The vibes her friends were giving off made her apprehensive.

"Don't worry about it." Ava said soothingly. "It'll be fine I promise." Zoe stepped through the hole in the fence and Ava gestured for Mia to follow. With significant reluctance, Mia stepped through the hole and Ava followed.

Thanks to a mysteriously unlocked window, the trio were navigating their way through the empty halls in a matter of minutes. The eerie blood-red crimson light of the setting sun gave the empty school an air of malice, and Mia felt a chill run down her spine as an unshakable dread gripped her.

They arrived at a particular classroom, also unlocked, and Ava turned the knob and led them in. The room was empty. The sanguine hue of the sunlight pouring in gave the interior of the classroom an otherworldly feel, as if they had somehow stepped into an alternate reality. Ava was the first to notice the lone boy at the back of the classroom.

"David, where is everybody?" Her tone made her annoyance and anger very evident. David Rineer, the star quarterback of the Penitent High football team, smiled.

Mia would forever remember that smile. It was far, far too wide for David's face, and incredibly malicious.

"What do you mean?" David asked calmly. "We're all here."

Ava was about to reply, but the words died in her throat as David's neck ripped apart. There was no blood, the flesh of his neck simply tore apart as if it was made of cloth.

Beneath Mia could see dark, scaly skin stretched over a lithe, serpentine neck. David's skin began to rip and tear apart like a costume that had suddenly become too small for its wearer.

His face split apart into three pieces and dropped away. Mia screamed when she saw the utterly inhuman muzzle beneath. A mouth filled to the brim with teeth like a shark, and snake-like fangs protruding from the upper maw.

A tail ripped free, and Mia saw an impossibly dark red flame flickering on its tip. The remains of the David disguise fell away, and standing before them was a reptilian monstrosity with scales the color of old, dried blood, a thick, powerful tail tipped with unnatural flame, a raptor-like body, twin arms emerging from its upper torso that looked just as capable of manipulating tools as tearing a human apart.

The whole hellish ensemble was topped with a head like a cross between a snake and a dog. Eyes burning with hellish fire glared at them with a hatred Mia couldn't even begin to fathom, and then the thing struck.

Ava fell screaming as the creature tore into her face. Its harrowingly sharp talons and mouth full of teeth split her chest open in seconds, and blood spurted everywhere, dousing her two shell-shocked companions.

The sound of a heartbeat filled the room, and Mia prayed it was her own heartbeat she was hearing. She snapped out of it first, grabbing Zoe's arm and dragging the still stunned girl back towards the door. The two burst out into the hallway and Mia had to drag the still dazed girl for a few seconds before Zoe got her wits back and the two girls took off at a dead run.

The blood-red light of the sun still streaming in through the windows now seemed to Mia like hideous foreshadowing, a sinister joke played on them by the demon they now fled from.

They ran mindlessly, out of panic, but when Mia realized this and started to search for the nearest exit, she suddenly found herself navigating halls utterly unfamiliar to her, a complete impossibility. Somehow, she and Zoe were now lost.

The sound of the heartbeat returned, and Mia felt a jangle of foreboding rattle up her spine. She turned back to see Zoe standing behind her, catching her breath in front of an open door leading to what must have been the gym. It was pitch-black inside except for a few beams of crimson light streaming in from the windows near the ceiling. With startled horror, Mia saw something dark and lithe move like a shadow through one of the sunbeams and screamed:

"Zoe watch out!" Zoe's cry of animalistic pain shook Mia to her core as the raptor-like jaws of the demon shot from the darkness to clamp down on Zoe's stomach. Blood welled from beneath the unholy vice of the demon's jaws and Zoe's piercing scream seemed all-encompassing.

Terrified, Mia watched her friend's spasming corpse be pulled back into the darkness by that gruesome, serpentine head on its long, tensile neck. Its fiery eyes burned with that same unquenchable hatred, and they stared into Mia's until they mysteriously vanished in the darkness of the gymnasium.

Mia fled with all she could muster. Her lungs burned and her legs screamed but still she ran. She knew if she ever stopped that thing would catch her. The blood red light of the sunset seemed to mock her, reminding her of her inevitable fate. Just when she felt like her lungs were going to burst and her legs were going to give out completely, she rounded a corner and saw the rear exit at the end of the hall.

On the other side of the doors, through the glass, she could see James walking towards her with concern and apprehension written all over his face.

She rushed towards him, ignoring his demands to know what had happened, and thrust herself into his arms, weeping and crying with unspeakable relief.

Recognizing extreme trauma when he saw it, James gripped her in a comforting embrace and tried to soothe her. Every time she felt like her tears would subside, the memories of her friends being torn apart by that creature came back and waves of uncontrollable sobs would gush from her as her tears stained her face with makeup.

She vaguely heard James calling emergency services on his phone, but he continued to embrace her with his free arm, gently rubbing her back while her tears soaked and stained his shirt.

What neither of them noticed was the slightly ajar door to the storage room at the other end of the hall, and the short, hook-nosed figure of Mr. Kaufman inside, holding a large, sharp knife dripping with blood.

Behind him, on the cold linoleum floor, was the mangled and blood-soaked body of David Rineer, his dark red blood gleaming in the crimson light streaming in from the solitary window.

ABOUT THE AUTHOR

J. R. Gawne

J.R. Gawne grew up in Kitchener, Ontario, the middle child of a three-child, middle-class suburban family.

Upon graduating from Cameron Heights Collegiate Institute he initially decided to pursue a career in the film industry, looking to follow in the footsteps of his role models George Lucas and Quentin Tarantino. When it became clear exactly what sort of environment and lifestyle that career path would lead him into, he opted to pursue writing to express his ideas instead.

He worked various industrial and factory jobs to support himself while he wrote his first works, and found unique inspiration in the experiences he had, relationships he formed, and the camaraderie he enjoyed with his co-workers while working "dirty jobs."

Most of his early works were published on various writing websites and forums under pseudonyms and received universal positive feedback, which encouraged him to take the leap of launching his career as an author. He enjoys writing horror, science fiction, and political thrillers, often combining all three genres into one.

He currently resides in the Rocky Mountains with his sister and her husband, as well as two dogs and three goats. He is on LinkedIn as J.R. Gawne and on Upwork as Joe G.

WHERE THE DEAD LIE

By Maya Scianna

I hate cemeteries.

I'd recently started to have to pass one every day on the way back from work at around midnight. Unfortunately, I didn't have a car, nor did I have any other means to pay rent.

My first job was in the opposite direction, and my second job that I had to recently get was on the opposite side. In addition, my stupid street was a dead end so I couldn't take any shortcuts. If I walked all the way around back from where I came from, I wouldn't be home until two in the morning, and my first job started at eight.

Every day the traffic light that was directly by the cemetery would take ages to turn, and I'd do my best to hold my eyes straight ahead, focusing on the white lines along the crosswalk. I'd started counting the lines across the street.

Eventually, I started counting how many seconds it took between the light changing and I could finally cross the street. Once I counted two-hundred and forty seconds before it finally changed.

One day, I'd lost track of counting when I'd heard shuffling from the bushes within the cemetery. I gulped and kept my eyes glued to the concrete beneath my feet, barely able to see the traffic light change.

I thought of the cat I'd once found nearby, and my mind was instantly at ease. Last I'd seen her, her dirt-covered white fur was falling out in little chunks around her belly and I could always see the outline of her bones. I'd started bringing cans of cat food just in case I'd run into her again, but I hadn't seen her since.

I thought about her big blue eyes and her friendly demeanor. My heart ached at the thought of something happening to her.

I reluctantly put my hands on the rusted black painted fence that encircled the cemetery and pulled myself high enough to get a better look. I examined the poorly maintained gravestones, the shrubbery around the sides of the gate, and overgrown tree roots that had tangled themselves over the rusted stones.

I sighed, hoping to see her white fur contrasting with the colors of nightfall. I decided that next time I saw her I was taking her home with me despite my apartment's rules about not having pets. I turned to go, ignoring the familiar pit in my stomach, reminding me that I was next to buried bodies, an area that I was once very familiar with.

Leaves crunched under my feet as I began to cross the street. Halfway through the crosswalk I turned and looked back at the cemetery, but was met with the face of a small child who stared back with a crooked grin. Her hair messily fell over her shoulders. Her eyes held mine, their grasp kept me there standing in the same spot where I had once tasted death.

My heart galloped in my chest and sweat gathered in the palms of my clenched hands. She turned away and walked with a limp and a crooked ankle that scraped against the concrete. She moved it in half circles as she used her working leg to pull her forward.

I rushed home, and the words repeated by my mother entered my head, *"As long as you don't acknowledge them, they can't get to you."*

I just happened to live by their resting place, a very significant one. The place I had to disturb every day by walking by it on the way to my retail job that I'd taken on in addition to my restaurant job since my mom was gone.

I turned on the shower and sat on the toilet lid, cupping my face in my sticky hands.

I stepped into the shower and let my hot tears mix with the mildly scalding water that poured down my face. I allowed myself to cry for those few minutes before putting on a brave face again.

"I see you."

I nearly slipped and lost my balance when I backed up against the wall. My eyes searched around frantically, and I opened the shower curtain, covering my body with it before shutting off the water. It had sounded as if the voice had been in there with me. It's slimy voice sent tingles up my spine.

I listened carefully, but my apartment was silent apart from the dripping water from both the showerhead on the porcelain tub floor, and my long hair onto the white tile. I snatched my coral pink towel from the hook beside the shower, I dried and wrapped myself in it before stepping out, then locked the bathroom door and listened carefully.

Drip. Drip. Drip. The sound began to drive me mad.

Childish giggles echoed through the bathroom. I grabbed my pink hairbrush off the sink. I knew it wouldn't help me, but the insignificant "weapon" I had in my grasp somehow made me feel better. Giggles echoed again, and it sounded like it was still coming from the shower. I shakily moved the shower curtain, looking from side to side and then downwards.

My eyes met a single one peering back at me from inside the drain, and skeletal fingers extended out of the drain and stretched out towards me. Black mold and sopping wet strands of hair were entangled around the bones and sharp ridges. I held back a scream and slammed my foot on the drain to close it. Unfortunately, the hand retracted back into the pipes within the drain before I could step on it.

I wanted to scream. I wanted it all to go away. Life had been so quiet until now. I slammed my hairbrush back on the sink, snapping the handle off. I clenched and unclenched my fists.

I looked at my blurred reflection in the foggy mirror. I could see the sunken in my eyes and dark circles that never left my face no matter how much sleep I obtained. I looked down at the pale skin on my arms and shoulders. I didn't always look this way.

The condensation on the mirror began to clear, and the water dripped down like wax on a lit candlestick, revealing a skull with pieces of skin hanging on by a thread. Dirt fell from my hair and eyes. I looked down and saw nothing but my towel and water droplets hitting the floor.

"Leave me alone!" I all but shouted the words and squeezed my eyes shut.

When I opened my eyes, my reflection had returned to normal. I raked my hands through my wet hair and tried to lower the tension in my body. I also avoided looking in the mirror again.

"You can't run forever" said a distant voice that seemed to echo in my head.

"Who said I'm running?" I replied with a shaky breath.

All I received in response was a distant cackling. Then the

bathroom lights flickered off.

I felt around the room for the light switch, first my hands met the wooden door, my memory signaled my hands towards the light switch that should have been to the left.

I traced my fingers along the textured wooden door and past the door frame until my middle finger and pointer finger found the light switch. It was still flipped on. I still attempted to switch it off and on before realizing that the power had gone out. I muttered a few curse words before remembering that my phone had a flashlight.

I slid my hands along the wall again. I traced the door and wall, feeling the slightly lifted and misshaped patterns until I was back by the porcelain bathroom sink where I'd set my phone in the corner, but it wasn't there.

I thought maybe I'd moved it somewhere else, but I wasn't sure where. I groaned, and again traced the wall back to the door, then unlocked and opened it. I wasn't sure what else I was supposed to do.

Everything was quiet except for the consistent sound of crickets chirping from the other side of the screen-covered window I'd left open this morning by accident. The sound was oddly relaxing. I basked in the comfort of the sound that echoed in the darkness where other things hid and leered in the corners unnoticed.

What happened next reminded me that I was not alone. The sound of breathing hit my left ear, and an icy breeze bit my skin as it raced by.

I squeezed my eyes shut and tried picturing bright skies with an endless field of roses. Unfortunately those visuals quickly shifted into a revolting face that had flesh barely holding to its jawbone and cheekbones.

It lay on the ground in front of a freshly dug grave. I watched as the scene of foliage grew out from below and pulled the decomposing body with it into the earth.

It was like watching a nightmare that you couldn't interact with unfold in front of you. I was forced to stare into the hollow face that had dry and wet pieces of mud holding on to both its flesh and bone before it was taken away. It was a reminder of who and what I really was.

I opened my eyes and the image disappeared, but I could have sworn that I'd heard distant laughter within the depths of my mind.

The lights flickered back on and the view of my cluttered apartment was illuminated around me. The view of the place I'd made my home for the past couple of months filled me with warmth and happiness. When my eyes landed on my mom's favorite sweater, my happiness faltered and my chest filled with grief. The lights flickered again multiple times, making a *buzzing* sound.

"This is wrong." A voice said in my ear. *"You cannot walk here anymore."*

"Why is that?" I ask, shuddering at the memory of a cold, eternal darkness that held me like a prison. I believed I knew the answer, but I wanted to be wrong. I thought of the face that appeared in my head. So familiar yet, not one I recalled ever seeing before today.

"Look at what you've caused," the world went dark, and my head filled with screams of terror and the familiar sound of a machine flat lining. One I'd heard before I'd woken up in an endless abyss.

"How many deaths has my life caused?"

"54."

My stomach churned with nausea and guilt. I didn't want to go back, but I felt conflicted with my morality. I thought about my mom's face when she held my hands that were caked in mud.

Tears were running down her face and landing on my shoulder as she stood there, hugging her only daughter that she'd lost to a semi-truck many years go. Even though time had past, she looked exactly the same as she did the night she'd lost me.

I also remembered her standing under the lamppost near the cemetery, her dark brown hair tied into a neat bun on the back of her head. She hadn't aged, but the world around her had. My memory of being dead was fuzzy, and I hadn't realized that I'd been anywhere other than that dark world of emptiness up until this point.

I closed my eyes and contemplated whether or not I was going to try and live the life my mom had wanted me to, or give in and save hundreds of lives that were disrupted in the balance. It wasn't a fair choice. It wasn't like I'd chosen to have a mother involved with dark magic and necromancy.

The lights *buzzed* and flickered back on as if nothing ever happened. I went to my closet and pulled out my favorite green sweater and jeans. At least this time I'd chosen what I died in.

Last time I was in a green hospital gown that was too big for my small body. I had to endure cold air on my back as I walked down the endless empty path that was the afterlife.

I stepped back outside and tiny strands of my wet hair crystalized in the freezing weather. The closer I got to the cemetery, the more I began to panic. My blood burned underneath my skin and my heart nearly leapt out of my chest. Sweat dripped down the sides of my face despite the temperature, but still froze onto my skin. I wiped my nose on my sweater and pushed forward.

The gates of the cemetery came into view as I climbed up

the hill. My hands and legs shook uncontrollably and I felt every part of my being telling me to run. I almost did.

I suddenly turned away, but as I had lifted my foot and was ready to sprint, I felt an invisible force pull me towards the cemetery. I dug one heel of my feet into the frozen dirt, and tried to use the other to get me to the sidewalk.

"You can't hold on forever" said the voice. I didn't answer, but I fought for my life for the one I'd lost. Within seconds I was holding onto the gates of the cemetery as I was pulled in. My hands burned as I held on, but I kept my grip as firm as I could. My muscles ached within my arms and shoulders as I held on. It wasn't long before my body gave out and my hands were ripped from the gate.

I hit the ground, my knee colliding with a rock beneath me in a dislocated position. I cried out in pain while I was continuously being dragged. Then it abruptly stopped.

I looked up, barely able to see through the tears in my eyes. I met the same eyes as I had earlier in the night, only this time I could see her clearly. Her features were defined by the bright light provided by full moon.

She had a round, pale face with bright green eyes that contrasted with her shoulder length dark hair. She appeared to be about sixteen years old. She glanced at me for a second before pulling her eyes back to the gravestone.

Her lips pulled into a small smile as she crossed out a name I couldn't quite read from a gravestone with a sharp rock that was similar to the shape of an arrowhead. Then she began carving something new into the rock, a name. My name. This was the girl my mother had put in my place to resurrect me. She took a poor innocent life in exchange for her own selfish desires.

I scrambled backwards and tried to pull myself to my feet,

but my knee gave out beneath me and I collapsed back to the ground. The girl didn't react to my sudden movements. I guessed she wasn't too concerned about me getting away.

I watched as the last letter of my name was etched into the stone, *Lindsey,* it read out. The girl dropped the sharp rock and dove for me with vengeful eyes and a triumphant smirk. She grabbed my ankles and pulled me with a strong force that I couldn't believe someone so small and frail could have.

I cried out for help, but by then my mouth filled with fresh dirt. My body was dragged through the dirt and into the grave as if the dirt was as soft as the first snowfall of the year.

Just as soft as the day I was stolen from life by an intoxicated driver. Except this time, I let go.

ABOUT THE AUTHOR

Maya Scianna

Maya is a freelance writer who enjoys writing fiction and invoking emotions within readers.

She mostly ghostwrites content for websites but will jump on the opportunity to write fiction stories, especially thrillers.

She currently has a website where she keeps a portfolio of stories she's written and a blog where she shares tips and her writing process.

When she's not writing, she's either reading, binging TV shows on Netflix, playing video games on her Switch, or looking for a new place to travel to.

You can reach Maya through her website: www.mscreative.online

Alternatively, her email is mayabree@gmail.com

ELSEWHERE

By Daniel Okotete

"Are you scared?"

The silence in the room, thick and vast; was suddenly broken by snores and giggles. Shadows danced here and there along with the movement of the dim candlelight.

McKenzie stared at the smiling faces of her sleeping roommates one by one. They looked happy.

They must be happy. So why? Why this unshakeable feeling? This fear.

She laughed nervously at her best friend. They had been friends even while they were still navigating through crawling and baby language.

Rosie had been an ugly baby. She only grew uglier as the years passed. As a teenager, mirrors made her cry.

Now as McKenzie stared at her perfect small face and short blonde hair, she looked every bit like a model.

There's nothing money can't buy, McKenzie thought as she stared at her new set of teeth glowing more than the only source of light in the room.

PING. . .PING

The sound told both girls that it was time. Rosie squeezed McKenzie's hands hard; it was her way of encouraging her friend.

"It's going to be okay Kenz. You know you can trust me. . . Trust us." She caught a sinister glint on the soft lines around Rosie's mouth as she bit off the last word. It was gone as soon as it appeared. Maybe she had imagined it. *Or maybe. . . No, no.* She had imagined it.

"Let's go," McKenzie said taking a deep breath, her eyes shut tight. "I'm ready."

"Are you sure Kenz?" Rosie squeezed tighter, her voice reflecting worry, her eyes two black holes swallowed by grimy essence.

"Yes! Just go already!" She implored, pulling her hands free.

Rosie waited just a while then grabbed her phone, unlocked it, and pressed the big button that glowed on the screen. Almost immediately, she fell back unconscious.

She looked peaceful, smiling just like the others.

McKenzie grabbed her phone and scrolled through. She saw the app. **ELSEWHERE. . .**

It was all everyone talked about and yet it was a secret. A visual world you enter when you sleep. Rosie had been begging her to join for months. She had refused for so long. It felt creepy as fuck.

Elsewhere. . .

Who names an app Elsewhere? And what's with the dream Voodoo stuff?

During the last few days, Rosie had gone from asking to begging till she had used their *sacred bestie bond promise*. The sacred bestie bond promise was *"Sacred"*.

Her finger hovered on **Uninstall.** *Do it! Get it over it!* Her heart slammed hard against her chest as her whole body quivered against her will. The silence wasn't helping. *The candle would soon die off. Just fucking uninstall it!*

The sound of a ping from her phone brought her back with a start. The big ENTER button glowed on her screen. She closed her eyes, praying silently to a God she hadn't spoken to since she left home.

She pressed the button.

The air burned with mist and dark energy. The walls on both sides were taut and wet. The enclosed darkness stretched far.

This didn't feel right. Was this how they welcomed new members? It was scary and it felt so real but she told herself it was all a dream. *Just a stupid realistic dream.*

She started walking slowly. The ground hummed with life. The earth below her feet thumped and pulsated with dark energy. Everything here oozed dark energy.

She could hear whispers and chatters coming from within the walls. Her eyes had started to adjust to the darkness. She could now make out the outline of her jeans and her outstretched hands which were trying to feel around.

Stopping, she moved closer to the wall on her right and listened; her ear close to the wet sticky wall. The voices were there, something else as well.

Movements.

She instinctively flinched. A feeling suddenly swarmed her almost frayed senses. A feeling that the walls were pulling closer.

Closer.

Heart thumping violently, McKenzie tore through the long hall full speed. She heard broken wails behind her. Surprised and somewhat relieved that she wasn't alone, she turned to find a silhouette.

A silhouette of a little child-like creature scurrying towards her. Shock scattered within her veins. Its movement was broken as joints, limbs twisted and contorted in every direction. It made sickening sounds as it advanced towards her. It was even scarier since she couldn't make out exactly what it looked like.

McKenzie increased her speed. Her eyes were wide with shock. Her heart felt like it was going to burst but she kept going.

She had to.

The creature was fast. Sounds of the evil cries getting closer, bones snapping and her frantic breathing filled the hall with echoes. It got so close that she could smell saliva and hunger radiating from deep within its core. The frenzied cries vibrated with primitive anticipation.

McKenzie saw the doorway only after she had entered the big space. The creature paused by the entrance unable to go further. It cried and screamed in obvious pain. Clicking its tongue, it skittered back into the welcoming hands of the darkness.

McKenzie fell to the dirt, hot tears burning her bruised skin. Everything hurt.

Everything.

Her chest felt like it was on a countdown to explode. This was getting all too real for a dream or a visual world. *Oh God, what have I done?*

They had given her some crappy tasting concoction to swallow and she had drunk it like the dummy she was. No questions, nothing. After all, the *sacred bestie bond's promise* was *sacred*.

Fuck!

Where are Gabby and Kiki?

The arrangement was they'd both come early to make sure everything was set for her first day in Elsewhere. Now she'd rather be anywhere else but here.

And where's Rosie?

Her tears intensified. They trickled freely, choking.

The sound of feet dragging made her aware of her surroundings. The space was in complete darkness. Darkness seemed to be the theme of this place, she noted.

She made a move to rise but stopped short as a figure shuffled past her. It reeked of death, of decay. She held back the urge to gag. Her stomach burned from fatigue and nausea.

The tall figure looked human yet it moved lifelessly, obeying no rational pattern of movement. McKenzie pulled herself to her knees staying low. She watched it close enough to tell it was somewhat human. The neck swiveled at an awkward angle. She couldn't make out the words that hissed out of the dead lips. She pushed closer.

"Help...Help me..." It repeated voicelessly.

She retreated in a crawl away from the figure. As she got up slowly, she whirled instantly and saw she was about to crash into another one.

Then another!

The place was crawling with them!

A thousand or so, drifting aimlessly while mumbling nothing in a speechless repetition. There was no space to turn. No space to move. No space to breathe!

No!

****

She woke up grudgingly. A part of her wanted to continue sleeping.

A big part of her.

Maybe if she was lucky, she'd wake up in bed just in time to see the girls arguing about their tv shows and men.

But a little part of her warned it was time to get up. Her raven-black hair clung to her skull. Everything here was wet. Her eyes were gradually adjusting to the gloom.

"ID." McKenzie turned around with a start.

A tall man was facing her. She assumed it was a man because of the thick male voice. Its features were absent. No hair on its head. No hair on its face. No eyes. No mouth. Its face was completely void. Its body was blank.

"Your ID?" the voice came out from the formless thing more like a command than a question.

McKenzie relaxed slightly. Certainly, this was part of the process to finalize her registration as a new member. She was going to drop her ratings to 2 stars. Anything lower would be genuine evil. That was when she noticed the lit doorway behind the blank form. Rosie and the girls must be there waiting for her.

She relaxed.

"ID number 421131." she let out evenly.

The formless thing looked harmless compared to the welcome crew she had met so far.

She relaxed further.

"Corrigan McKenzie?" the thing asked in the same commanding tone.

She nodded. McKenzie looked above its head to the lit doorway again. There was something painted there. It looked fresh.

MUICIFIRCAS.

Sounds like an exotic drink or something. A warning light in the back of my mind came on but she dismissed it immediately.

"What's your name?" She asked because the silence was starting to break down the little peace she was beginning to build since entering this world.

"I have no name," the creature said to her maintaining its thick tone.

"Well, now you're Blanky," she said with a pout, head cocked.

Nothing. No reply.

Someone wasn't good at keeping conversations.

She looked up. **MUICIFIRCAS**. The warning light blinked rapidly.

"Blanky, where are my friends?" she asked determined on making sure the silence didn't exist at all; head cocking further.

"Partying. With their friends."

Her friends were partying with their friends which were about to be her friends because she was about to meet them; if eventually, this lump of boredom showed her the way on time for the party she was missing at this moment.

Maybe 2 stars was showing mercy after all. "And what exactly am I doing here?" the irritation in her voice shocked her.

"Waiting."

Waiting? Waiting?

It took everything she had to make herself relax. The vein on her temple looked ugly. Her eyes moved up and kept. **MUICIFIRCAS**. Something about the word sent cold chills down her long spine.

SACRIFICIUM. No. She was imagining things.

"Blanky," her voice was a croak. "Shouldn't I be at the party with my friends?"

"No."

Her heart heaved at the word, flat and impassive.

"Why?" McKenzie's voice sounded more like a plea than a question.

"I think you already know," the thick voice hit her core, splitting her composure into fragments.

Her mouth dropped in horror. *Sacrificium*. Her Latin was rusty but she knew.

Sacrifice.

Her mouth fell.

"Don't scream. You'll expire," it came out more like a gentle warning.

Her hands instinctively flew to her mouth stifling the echoes of her pain to soundless whimpers. McKenzie dropped to the ground folding into a fetal position. Her tiny frame trembled with heavy sobs.

The people she called her friends had offered her up to this wicked app and she would die alone in this demonic place! Her tears burned her throat making breathing impossible. Rosie had been everything to her. They had been everything to each other. Then there was the *sacred bestie bond.*

Screw that.

McKenzie thought about her mom. Jenna had always warned her about these types of things. McKenzie had seen it as ridiculous superstition and now. . . McKenzie was the one closest to her mom. Her sister lived in her job. No one ever saw her or heard from her. She cried knowing she'd never see her mom again or her twin. She cried hard.

Some minutes later, McKenzie struggled to her feet wobbling over to Blanky. She looked up at the hideous form devoid of everything that makes a person human. *What if it had once been a person just like her?* She held the smooth blank hands.

"Can I ask for one thing before we go?" Her voice flat and emotionless held brutal strength.

Blanky's head moved for the first time, his featureless face pointing down towards her. She held back a giggle. Maybe he had been too much of a bore in life that his features had run off for greener pastures. She laughed hard.

****

The big house was devoid of its residence except for the woman in the kitchen humming with a vibrant smile. A string of graying hair fled from the net on her head. With one deliberate motion, the strands disappeared back into their prison.

The polished marble walls revealed the wealth of the owner, the scent of baking refreshing the air with homely warmth. Initially, she had been terrified of the thought of staying alone in this fortress.

She had thrown parties and hosted meaningless meetings just to keep the house from feeling like a cage. She had even taken home a guy or two on some occasions when the nights got unbearable and lonely.

Common sense had cautioned her quick on the dangers of continuing this path. A rich old woman alone in this palace of comfort was the most vulnerable target so she found a substitute for the lost company.

Baking. She liked the aroma it brought to the house and the feeling of flour against her wrinkled skin. She liked the look on the faces of the youngsters next door when they saw her walking down the porch with her basket of goodies.

Yes, this no longer felt like Fort Charlie. Her heart ached as she remembered her baby girl. McKenzie had been like her sister; unlike her actual twin McKenna.

Going to school had been hard on both mother and child. While McKenna had just left one day for the army. As she hummed the last verse of the famous country song, Jenna noticed she still hadn't gotten the call from Kenzie. She usually phoned after classes. That was supposed to be 2hours ago.

Maybe she finally met a boy. The girl had been a slave to her studies for so long. Jenna smiled at the thought of her baby finding a boy.

As Jenna mixed the last batch with care and patience of her age, the light fluttered.

She paused.

Nothing ever went wrong with electricity here except during maintenance. She resumed her work reluctantly, eyes darting to the light bulb in-between stirs. Just when she was finally regaining her equilibrium, the light gave out. She froze.

The rest of the house appeared to be working fine.

Dropping the spoon, she groped her way shakily to where she knew the switch would be. She jabbed it like a calculator verifying it no longer worked. Her hands went to her throat instinctively.

Fear yanked her spine. She struggled in the darkness shuffling groggily towards where the door should be. Reaching the doorway, cold bit at her nostril making her exhale a cloud of smoke. She used her mouth; expelled cold mist.

Her heart kicked out. She had read the books and understood the signs of sorcery. Her hands shook at her throat as she felt her body go stiff with fear. Jenna wanted to scream but nothing came out.

As she got close to crossing the door, a force threw her back gently slamming the door shut. The room vibrated from the shock wave. Jenna's breath caught in choking gasps. The darkness was suffocating, the cold stabbing her with talons of fear.

She started backing away from the door her eyes never leaving the oak frame. Never blinking. The tap on her shoulder caused her legs to wobble. Jenna was going to pass out. She would likely die from a heart attack before this witch had the opportunity of harvesting and eating her organs.

She turned gradually, the hands on her neck as white as her hair. Standing there was McKenzie white and unearthly. She looked transparent, less human than the tall man beside her.

The man staring without eyes or mouth or hair. Jenna fell to the ground, eyes locked on her child. A warm smile brushed the pale lips of the apparition in front of her that resembled her baby girl.

The smile McKenzie always gave her specially. The smile that said, "hey momma" without words. McKenzie always called her momma. The tall form gave an impatient grumble.

The pale figure of her daughter strolled hesitant to Jenna. Jenna tried to speak but the effort only made her cry. It even smelled like McKenzie; Coco and something warm. Jenna's tears blurred the world.

"*They killed me, Momma. The girls. Rosie an—.*"

The light was back. The odor of burnt croissant swallowed the room entirely. The only thing out of place now was the crying woman on the floor pale and trembling violently.

ABOUT THE AUTHOR
Daniel Okotete

Daniel Okotete was born in 1995 in Delta State, Nigeria.

Growing up, he was fascinated with rapping, and this interest led to some early exposure to reading and writing since he was drawn to words.

Later, Daniel studied art and philosophy and now he teaches history at college level.

He studies mythologies in his free time and has been able to write some novels mostly mystery and horror books.

DRINKS PROVIDED

By Coward Huntington

The room where I was sitting could have been any room, in any building, anywhere - but it wasn't.

Grey paint covered every inch. The floor was a drab polished linoleum. The only furniture present was the small table and the uncomfortable chair where I sat.

I took a deep breath. My fingers were still shaking. I could hear the faint buzz of a camera pointed straight at me.

The Police had found me in the midnight, running as fast as my legs could carry me. They had pulled their car in front of me; the headlights burning through the fog.

As the pair left the vehicle I remained frozen stiff, the headlights basically paralyzed my whole body. I was still wearing my ridiculous sweatshirt and older brother's sneakers that didn't fit me.

The cop's boots crunched against the falling snow. The taller one slipped a pair of glasses over her eyes, the other twirled a thick red mustache.

"Okay son," said the tall officer, "Where abouts do you think you're headed this late at night?"

My jaw chattered.

I knew they had their eyes pressed onto me, but I couldn't help it. I had to keep looking over my shoulder into the swirling black behind me. Just in case I was still being followed. By, those - *those things*...

The cops drew closer, their faces more serious.

Then I answered. I told them the truth. I told them I was out looking for *them*.

That was only hours ago.

Rapid memories bounced around in my head, only interrupted by the sound of a creaking door in the corner.

Both the cops entered the interview room without a word, big dark glasses still obscuring their eyes.

"So." the mustached cop growled, "Again. The story. From the beginning."

I stared down at my fingers on the plain table before me. My body was still, but my heart pounded in my ears, so hard that I thought I might explode at any moment.

My mind raced, I calmed the storm in my head, and spoke.

It had all started with a pizza.

That's right, a regular steaming-hot pizza. To be specific, a large Margarita with extra olives.

When the doorbell had rung, I was too busy glued to my laptop to hear it. I had been watching TV for so long I had completely forgotten that I ordered. So when my brother Paul entered the room, I jumped.

"Pizza for dinner... *Again?*" he said, "Your blood's going to be straight cheese soon, Jim."

He dropped the steaming Margarita onto the fold-out couch.

I snapped towards it like a ravenous dog.

My brother was dressed in a fancy suit, a silk shirt. He'd slicked his hair back. When he'd first met me at the train station earlier that week, it had shocked me to see him like that. At home, he had always been a more casual kind of guy, popular, always out partying. By now, I was used to it. Paul was always at work.

"You don't have anything else to do tonight?" Paul asked.

"Like what?" I said, a mouthful of cheese.

"I don't know," he said, "*It's Friday!* Surely you don't want to just do this every night. You came to the city for a reason, right?"

I shrugged.

I didn't know anyone out here, but the truth was the situation was similar back at home, too. Not that I didn't like people, or didn't have friends. I just didn't like parties. I never liked the way people act in social situations. Their personalities would shift, like they had turned into different beings, all the same as each other. Repeating the same things, dancing the way everyone else approved, even laughing the same.

Paul shook his head and leaned onto the arm of the sofa bed, grabbing a slice.

"It's a big city," Paul said, "Lots of people you could meet. I don't know, *you do you.*"

He smacked his lips, grunting approvingly at the pizza, throwing the half-eaten slice back in the box.

"Well," I said, "What are *you doing?*"

"Lobster," Paul said.

He turned towards the hall, smiling when he saw the dumbfounded expression on my face.

"I got a dinner, Jim." He said, "Work-stuff."

I found myself on my feet, crumbs falling at my feet.

"On a Friday?" I said.

In the hall, Paul nodded and opened the door. Outside his apartment, the snow curled over the black night behind it.

"But you don't even like lobster!" I called.

A smile curled around my brother's face.

"Sometimes you gotta follow the herd, Jim."

The door slammed behind him.

I spent a moment chewing on a mouthful of cheese. The room suddenly felt empty. I shrugged and found my place back on the fold-out couch, staring at my empty computer screen.

Suddenly, my phone buzzed.

The freezing night air burned my skin. I trudged through the snow, severely underdressed. I had thrown on any of Paul's old clothes I could find in the bottom of his drawers.

I still wasn't sure who had messaged me or how they got my number. When I had asked, the same message had repeated itself, with the exact same wording.

If you're reading this, you have been chosen. No dress code. Drinks Provided.

Below read coordinates. They had led me to a spot middle of the woods on the edge of town. As I closed in on the endless dark trees, I instantly wished I had brought warmer clothes. Snowflakes melted on my skin. I couldn't smell anything but smoke and the entire area was quiet but for the whipping of the wind through the black trees.

I stepped, one frostbitten step at a time. My blue fingers trembling over my phone, checking my bearings.

Had Paul given someone my number? I couldn't be sure, but the mysterious message had my mind swirling. The butterflies in my stomach drew me closer, but my heart was still sitting on that couch, wrapped in the blanket in the warmth of Paul's apartment.

In that moment, I promised myself I would give it just fifteen minutes. If by the time that passed I was still feeling nervous, then I would go straight home - no questions asked.

After all, I didn't know who these people were. They wouldn't remember me. They wouldn't remember *anyone.* They would be just thinking about themselves, worried about fitting in, about being the same as everyone else.

Suddenly, the blue dot on my phone that was me hovered over the location. I stopped walking.

I looked up at the night sky. Through the swirling of the leaves, I made out nothing but falling snow. Around me, the entire forest was dead silent. I was alone. A fear started building in my stomach, suddenly I began spinning. Looking around at the trees all around me. There was no one to be seen.

What had I done? Here I was, standing in the middle of the woods, ready for whatever psychopath was eyeing me from the dark.

Then I noticed another sound, a thumping. It was coming from right below me.

I looked down.

Under the snow was a trapdoor. I brought my freezing fingers to the metal grate and revealed the empty dark beneath a cold steel ladder leading into the black. The sound of hollow voices awaited me.

Fifteen minutes, I told myself. I set my alarm.

When I entered the abandoned drain, I found the place alive with the flames of many candles and the occasional flashing disco light. Many shadowy figures hung around the great cement space. Eerie music was pumping from some cheap-looking speakers charging on a generator. A light mist from the cold outside drew in from the end of the tunnel that glowed with faint moonlight.

I shivered, stepping forward.

A young woman spun to meet my step. She was cute, and her clothes were bright and full of crazy colors, but her face was still, her eyes somewhat milky and blank.

"I'm so glad I was chosen." She placed a red cup in my hand.

I glanced down; it was full of some translucent liquid. I've never been much of a drinker, but I accepted it in my hand, my trembling fingers carrying the cup as she led me towards a group of partygoers in the circle nearby.

I eyed my drink as the group introduced themselves. They all seemed like nice people. They had all come from all different walks of life, and told me of their lives, but they all carried the familiar numbness, the big-city emptiness I had seen consuming my brother.

Their eyes were blank and gray, their faces all pressed on me. "Have a drink." they would occasionally stretch a finger towards my cup.

A chill ran down my spine.

All their gray eyes fixed on me, or should I say, *beyond me.*

"I'm going to go for some air," I said.

"I'm so glad you were chosen," said the girl.

I frowned, and shrugged off the comment, looking down at my feet as I walked towards the moonlight.

The frost met me at the end of the tunnel. I crouched down on a rock and checked my messages. Out in the drain's exit the trickling water ended in a small pond. I shivered. It was swimming with strange-looking tadpoles.

My reception was out. I held it to the moon.

The party had been about as I expected, but being out and talking with the group had brought a strange energy to me. I decided I would call Paul, maybe even meet him somewhere. When he was finished, maybe we could even grab a drink together.

Something sloshed in my cup. I turned my eyes down towards my drink.

Weirdly, one tadpole had made its way into my cup. It seemed impossible. I gazed down at the strange creature, struck by its curious pale gray eyes. They seemed familiar.

The sound of crunching feet filled the surrounding air.

I looked up, realizing; the group had followed me. A chill ran down my spine as I took in the sight of the partygoers slowly forming a silent circle around me, eyes blank.

"Hey guys," I said.

"Did you drink?" asked the girl.

I looked down at my cup, then down at the pond and the weird tadpoles below me.

What happened next, I will never forget until the day I die. The sight of what I saw sent a chill through my whole body. The group in the reflection looked different, *horrible.* Their bodies were the same, but in the water's gleam I could see their true faces. Ghastly, terrible faces covered in slime, swimming with rage, milky gray eyes fixed on me. Same as the tadpole that swum around in my cup.

My phone suddenly came alive with messages. News reports, missed calls, and a message from Paul.

Don't leave the house.

An ice cold hand landed on my shoulder.

"I'm-" I started, "I'm so glad I was chosen."

Their eyes stayed fixed on me.

"Then drink." The girl said.

She had called my bluff. I brushed off the ice in my veins and managed an award smile, bringing the paper cup slowly to my lips.

The group fixed horrible eyes on me, watching as I drank. Their bodies ready to strike, their faces full of anticipation.

I felt the weird tadpole thing inside my mouth, swishing past my tongue and diving for my throat.

The mist was creeping in from all sides. I saw something glimmer past the trees.

A highway.

Suddenly, my phone alarm exploded, and the group froze.

I spat the liquid with all my might, and before I could take a breath, I was running as fast as my oversized shoes could take me.

The dark trees whipped by my step. Those *things* were everywhere I looked, running with lightning fast intensity, their faces remaining slack. I don't know how I ran so fast, but I kept going. The pizza churned in my stomach. My legs felt like they were burning, yet still forwards I went until I could move no more.

I stopped, the slick highway alive with frost. I took the deepest breath I could manage.

A roaring sound followed. I turned.

Headlights were blinding me.

"So that's it." The officer dropped his pen.

I nodded.

My fingers shook on the plain table. Repeating the story, I still couldn't believe what I had seen. I wished for the safety of Paul's sofa-bed, the crumbs and the warm blanket.

"And your brother?" asked the taller officer. "Did you get to speak to him?"

"No," I said, "I didn't have a chance to tell anyone yet."

The police had taken my phone when they brought me in. The officers looked up at the corner of the room, waving a hand. The buzzing of the camera suddenly stopped.

My heart ran still.

"*Perfect,*" she said.

I tried to move.

With all my strength, *I tried.*

It was too late. I was already frozen in fear in my chair as the officers stepped closer.

In one, unanimous moment, they pulled the dark glasses away.

Cold gray eyes fixed on me.

ABOUT THE AUTHOR

Coward Huntington

Inspired by surreal storytellers like Kathy Acker, Haruki Murakami and David Lynch, Thomas "Coward" Huntington publishes independent novels in the genre of Weird Fiction, Horror and Magic Realism. With his work he explores the issues and anxieties of the 21st Century, joining a new wave of emerging independent authors.

Born in Melbourne, now based in Berlin, Coward Huntington has been writing since he was young. He works freelance as a full-manuscript ghostwriter, specializing in Fantasy, Adventure and Romance.

He also works as an SEO copywriter and editor with an Advanced Diploma in Media. Coward takes pleasure and pride in writing stories that stick. In a world with an ever expanding amount of writers, it takes a lot to find stories that resonate. Coward's blog, Third Drawer Stories, promotes the stories fiction writers can't find a home for. From the strange to the surreal, to the downright absurd, Coward provides them a home, paired with visceral imagery to match from local artists.

If you would like to know more about Coward personally, tune into Opheads. Coward and friends podcast invites you to take a second look at the world of media. It covers the stories that matter to you and the truth that lies behind the headlines.

BOOKS AND CREATIVE PROJECTS: www.cowardspace.com

GHOSTWRITING & CREATIVE SERVICES: www.thomashuntingtonwrites.com

MAIL LIST & UPDATES: Join my mailing list to receive a free copy of my novella Drosophila!

THE BESTSELLER

By David Phiri

You've probably heard about it by now. It shouldn't have made it the way that it did; it wasn't even my best work. But it hit big, it reached too many eyes. I'm so sorry to everyone I hurt, it was me. My name is Matt Colton, and I stole the story. I deserve all the punishment.

You have to understand why I did it so callously. I had a shitty job in a tiny town. When I wasn't on shift I was bent over my laptop trying to write something, anything, but nothing would come and I would barely get any sleep that day and every other day.

I was wasting away, living like a zombie, wandering from home to work in a brain-dead trance every single day. I lived alone, I had no friends, no relationships, not even parents or families. My father died before I was born and my mother died two years ago, neither of their families cared about me so I was all alone. I was running on fumes. I needed to do something.

One day a strange short man walked into the gas station store I work at. He had a strange gait to him, like he was limping slightly.

He was wearing a long tattered coat with a hood over his head and he was whispering to himself as he crossed the aisles. I kept a close watch on him. He looked like the sort that would pull a gun on me. But there was a shotgun under the register, pointed towards the customer side. I doubted it was legal but I made sure I had one hand there when he made his way over.

He got some snacks and some drinks. I noticed he was scratching loudly at his neck, so loud that you could hear the flesh peeling off him. It's a disturbing sound that, to this day I'm not entirely rid of it. It is like listening to a spoon being raked across a pan.

I noticed that he had gashes running down his neck where he was scratching. I said nothing. The sooner he left the better my life was. He would be pretty hard to forget. When he left the store he dropped a square looking black object into the trash can outside.

Naturally, I dug that shit up. You can say I'm a curious guy. What kind of loner with an acute diagnosis of main character syndrome isn't? I love chasing dumb risks. What's the worst it could be; maybe he had a disease that could kill me in days. Who gave a fuck? I was already suicidal,

The book was normal enough. There were pages and pages of scrawled out passages that were unreadable. But the last page had it. The story. It was simple in truth.

In the story, a man goes to sleep and he's visited by a demon named Palos that tells him that it'll grant him any wish as long as he claws his eye out. The story tells how the man makes his choice and agrees to the demon's deal.

The guy's theory is that he can wish himself back to good health once it is done. But it kills him. The thing was a cruel joke. So of course I submitted that into the leading horror website in the world.

I'd been rejected so many times by that point that I put it out of my mind and forgot about it.

I got a call the next week saying that the thing had amassed ten million viewers. You see, the site paid per view. The story was crushing. It was the biggest thing on the site and even Stephen King had published stories there.

That was how crazy it all was. I did interviews on TV. I was invited to conventions. I sold the short story in a collection with other things I'd written over the years. Nobody cared about anything else. It was all about that short story, that bestseller. It changed everything.

I moved out of the rundown apartment I was staying in and bought myself a beautiful condo in the Texas suburbs. I had more people paying attention to me, I was invited to parties, when I spoke people listened, especially when it was about horror. I was someone now. One night I burned the book, to put it behind me and make my own mark in the world.

I set it off.

I live alone. So when I heard the knock at my slightly parted bedroom door I was surprised. I was met with a scene that confused me for a second.

I'd just woken from a deep slumber so I was surprised to be seeing eyes on top of eyes on top of eyes and bodies lying on each other at my bedroom door. They weren't moving, they were staring at me while completely motionless.

Their skins looked like they'd been burned to black. There must've been ten people crowded around my door. I leapt out of my balcony. They found me the next day. A concerned neighbor noticed my body on the ground.

"You are stressed," The therapist told me after a few days in recovery. "You are tired, this sort of thing happens quite often to people with insomnia like you. It can even be exasperated if those people are writers or creators of some kind. It's easier for them to hallucinate. The lack of sleep makes it so difficult for them to distinguish between what is real and what is not. What is a dream and what is reality?"

"That doesn't explain the footprints." I said.

Ash-grey footsteps were found on the wooden tiles outside my bedroom door. The police started looking into the case for me. Their suspicion was that I was the target of a group of pranksters. But I remembered those people. They had skin that looked like it had been charred black like coal.

All of them had one eye. You can't fake that. But the police case was what uncovered it. The foot prints matched those of victims from cold cases, who were found dead with pieces of their bodies extracted. Some people were missing fingernails, others toes or fingers, but all of the victims were missing an eye.

The cops believed it was a group of people responsible. The victims would leave behind messages dating back to a week before their murders, talking about demons watching them sleep.

I didn't know what to think and neither did anyone else. The police kept looking at me strangely but they couldn't deny that I had nothing to do with it because I was in hospital during several of the latest killings. Whoever these people were, they weren't stopping.

What was the source of the craze? Could it be a drug? A group of killers moving from place to place? There were so many questions.

But I knew one thing for sure. I couldn't go back home. I tried to make them keep me at the hospital for as long as possible. But eventually they told me I had to go back home. But because of the murders, I was being guarded the whole time by police officers. There was usually at least one in the house and at least two officers outside the house as well, armed and ready.

It didn't matter. I couldn't sleep. For days I could barely blink at night, afraid that they would come for me. I slept with the light on.

That night though, my lights flickered and one of the cops in my house went down to check the breaker.

"It should be working, there's nothing wrong." He put his radio to his lips. "Any movement out there?" The cop outside gave him the all clear. There was nothing wrong.

But I couldn't stop trembling from head to toe.

I lay down in my bed. One of the cops was in the room adjacent to mine. There was a bed in there and before long I could hear him snoring. I couldn't sleep. I got up and started pacing from one end of the room to the other. But something stopped me dead in my tracks.

Outside the window, among the trees outside, I spotted the man I stole the book from. His hood was down, his eyes were fixed on mine. He was looking right at me, but there was something right beside him. It was harder to see…or rather, it was harder to make sense of than the man.

A bulbous creature, it looked like it was made of flesh, but inside out. It was writhing and swelling up.

"They're out there!" I called to the police officers. "Help!" I tried to run but I tripped over something and felt wetness on my feet.

When I looked down I found the cop that was supposed to be in the other room licking my foot. But the way he was laying there…it was wrong, he had no shoulders, it was just his head.

From the looks of him his neck had been ripped right off. The muscle and sinew of skin looked ragged. A clean cut would look neat.

I screamed, as the muscles in my limbs tightened and froze from my heart hammering fear. I couldn't move. I heard laughter all around me, on every side, everywhere I turned. That was when I noticed them all.

The people with the scorched black skin. Their eyes staring down at me without blinking. They surrounded my room, naked as the day they came into the world. The decapitated cop's tongue kept gliding up and down my toe too.

By the time the man came up with the demon, I was as stiff as a block of ice.

"It is a pleasure to finally meet you. I am Rodrigo. You took my pain." The man whispered. His wounds were healed. "You stole from me. That wasn't yours to show the world. Look what you've done now, but Palos is quite agreeable to deals. You have ten fingers, ten toes, rows and rows of teeth. There is enough pain on you for him to wipe the slate mankind owe him clean."

But I wasn't moving. There was no way I would harm myself.

Rodrigo stood and the bulbous creature, Palos, approached, now that it was up close I could see the eyes. Eyes that had been ripped out of their sockets clung loosely to the mangled shape of the bulbous flesh being.

"You see the reports are wrong." The short man continued, though my eyes were transfixed on the monster I could hear him scratching at his neck. "Those people they found dead. None of them did any of that by choice. In the story, the deal only comes if you pull your own eye out, and even then, you still have to survive it or the deal is void because you are dead."

I felt a tingle in my hand as it rose of its own accord like I was a puppet in a play. I couldn't stop it.

"How about we just take a nail tonight, Palos?" The man asked the flesh monster. To me, he said, "He likes to make you suffer in anticipation. He's one of the gods of pain, you see. But not really the physical kind, he's all about torment."

My hand was thrust into my mouth. I felt my teeth close on one of my fingers. Despite the effort I put in, whatever hold the monster had on me was too strong. My teeth closed on the nail of my index finger. The nail left my finger with a sickening rip. Pain burned all over my hand.

I have no idea what happened to the monsters, I was found on the floor the next day. The cops that were in the house to protect me had tortured themselves before dying and removed an eye, each of them, even the decapitated one, with their bare hands.

I confessed to all of the murders. I just wanted to be locked up in the most secure dark hole they could find. I told them that I would do it again and again. The truth was that I would do it. To be locked up in a place where they couldn't get me, I would try anything.

During the whole process I was never visited once by Rodrigo and Palos. But the day I was transferred to my cell after they finally found me guilty, there it was again. The book. How was it there? I'd burned the damn thing.

On the desk where they let inmates place their possessions. The little black book was there waiting for me. I screamed for them to let me out but the guards beat me to a pulp and spat on me. They were looking for a reason to do it, they thought I was a killer.

There was no evidence I did anything of course, but they believed I organized it all.

That night when the cells were dark and the other inmates were asleep. I heard the sound of feet slapping on concrete. There it was again. Dotted with eyes around its fleshy body, it was more manlike now, as if it had molded itself to a man like shape. On top of its mangled shape, like a crown on the beast's head, was the dismembered body of Rodrigo. But the eyes were open and seeing, the lips curled into a smile.

I couldn't take it anymore. So I did it. My nails pressed into the flesh around my eyes and I dug them both out. As the blood leaked out of my eyes, I laughed. *Free at last,* I thought to myself.

ABOUT THE AUTHOR
David Phiri

David Phiri was born and raised in Johannesburg, South Africa, but currently resides in Manchester, England.

After enduring a tricky time in a finance degree, he traded business, money and security to focus all his attention into bringing the grim characters in his mind to life in Fantasy, Horror and Science-Fiction stories.

He is the winner of the 2020 edition of the Keith Fletcher Memorial Access to HE Prize. When he isn't writing, he is trying to be a better musician and planning a dream trip around the world.

CHECK OUT THESE TITLES

Creepy Nightmares

Horror Stories To Tell In The Dark: Book 1, 2, 3, 4

Scary Short Stories For Teens: Book 1, 2 & 3

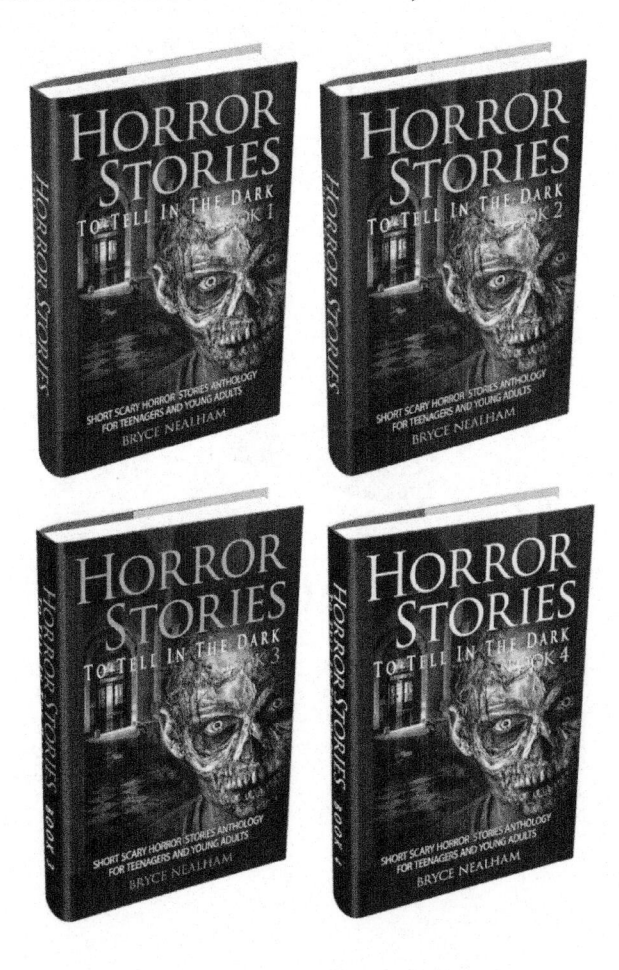

MORE ➡

HORROR STORIES TO TELL IN THE DARK: BOOK 3

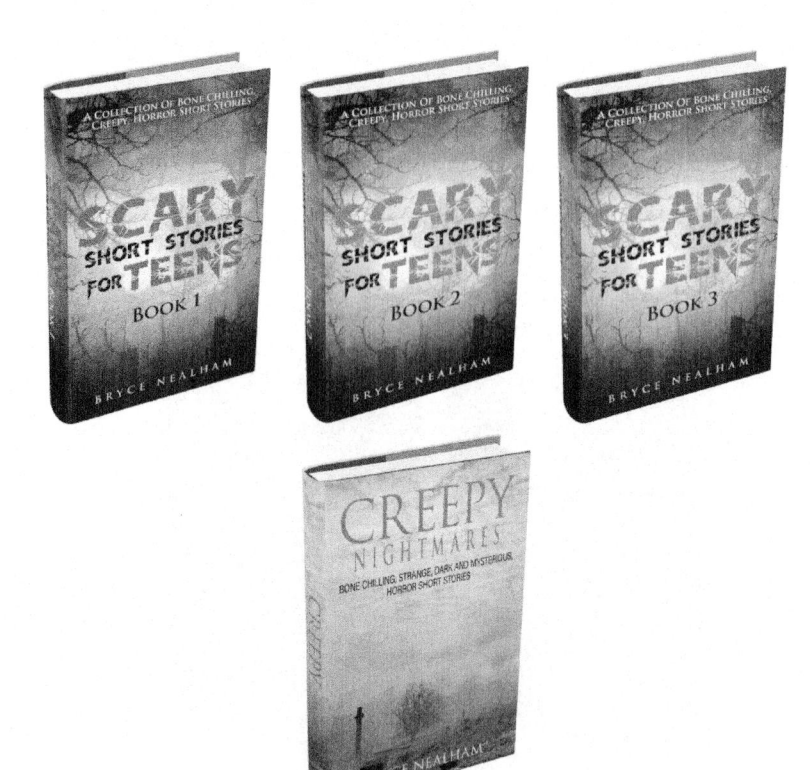

MORE COMING SOON!

Printed in Great Britain
by Amazon